To my three little dragons, Justin, Connor, and Joelle, for always keeping me on my toes. Thank you for the precious gift of motherhood.

www.mascotbooks.com

So You Want a Pet Dragon?

©2020 Tania Pourat. All Rights Reserved. No part of this publication may
be reproduced, stored in a retrieval system or transmitted in any form
by any means electronic, mechanical, or photocopying, recording or
otherwise without the permission of the author.

For more information, please contact:
Mascot Books
620 Herndon Parkway #320
Herndon, VA 20170
info@mascotbooks.com

Library of Congress Control Number: 2019920704

CPSIA Code: PRTWP0720A
ISBN-13: 978-1-64543-234-0

Printed in South Korea

so you want a
Pet Dragon?

Tania Pourat

Illustrated by Tristan Tait

So you want a pet dragon?

It sounds like a lot of fun. But oh boy, it's hard work.

You see, dragons have short tempers and get easily angered. That's why it's super important to keep your dragon calm at all times.

How do you do that? you might ask. Well...

First, you have to start
each day with a big,
wholesome breakfast.
A hungry dragon is
an angry dragon.

When it's time to leave the house, be sure your dragon is dressed in comfortable clothing so they don't get itchy.

A daily yoga session
is absolutely necessary
to release stress.

Regular massages will help
your dragon unwind.

Essential oils are needed to
make sure your dragon can relax.

You'll also need to take your dragon on vacation to exotic places to give them a break every now and then.

Dragons need plenty of exercise
to use up their energy.

You also need to exercise their mind with long eating—whoops, I mean reading—sessions.

Speaking of eating, don't forget to keep the snacks rolling throughout the day.

You can't do too much every day.

Dragons need lots of free time to play with friends and be a little silly.

After a long day,
your dragon will
surely need a
warm bubble bath.

Be prepared with
cookies and milk as well.

Last but not least, there is nothing like a story at bedtime to get your dragon ready to sleep after a long day.

Let's face it.
Owning a dragon is no
walk in the park, but it
sure is worth it!